This Book Belongs To:

_____

Donated by
The Little Bit Foundation

THE
little bit
FOUNDATION

1·2·3·READ!

THE LITTLE BIT FOUNDATION

When the Earth Wakes

Ani Rucki

Scholastic Press · New York

Library of Congress Cataloging-in-Publication Data   Rucki, Ani.   When the Earth wakes / Ani Rucki. — 1st ed.
p.   cm.   Summary: Accompanied by bears, the Earth wakes in spring, plays in summer, gets sleepy in fall, and goes back to sleep in winter.
ISBN 0-590-05951-3   [1. Seasons—Fiction. 2. Earth—Fiction. 3. Bears—Fiction.] I. Title.
PZ7.R831455Wh   1998   [E]—dc21   97-8187   CIP   AC
10 9 8 7 6 5 4 3 2 1   8 9/9 0/0 01 02 03 Printed in the U.S.A.   37   First edition, February 1998
The text type for this book was set in Senza Black.
The illustrations are Berol Prismacolor Pencils on black illustration board.
Book design by Kristina Iulo

This book is dedicated to
the art-filled eyes of my mom
and the art-filled hands of my dad.
Thank you for sharing with me.
And to Kevin Lewis, writer extraordinare.

When the earth
wakes in spring...

...she throws off her snowy blankets,

and dances with
fresh, soft breezes.

By the time
summer arrives...

...she is wide awake
and full of life.

She heats up and thunders
through long, hot days

into bright and noisy nights.

...the earth
becomes
drowsy.

She drapes herself
in colorful leaves

and gets ready for winter.

**And it is then,
shaken by cold winds...**

...that she covers herself

with blankets of snow

and drifts into a deep, quiet sleep

and dreams until spring.